SMELLY
This ~~Little Tiger~~ book belon

D0246095

This book is dedicated to everyone who has ever laughed at their own trumps!

Also, special thanks to my sister, Lynn, for the hours spent co-editing, travelling by train between London and Liverpool. And thanks to Kate for all the finishing touches.

LITTLE TIGER PRESS
An imprint of Magi Publications
1 The Coda Centre, 189 Munster Road, London SW6 6AW
www.littletigerpress.com

First published in Great Britain 2004
This edition published 2005

Text and illustrations copyright © David Roberts 2004
David Roberts has asserted his right to be identified
as the author and illustrator of this work under the
Copyright, Designs and Patents Act, 1988
All rights reserved

A CIP catalogue record for this book is available
from the British Library

Printed in Belgium by Proost NV

ISBN 1 84506 011 3

4 6 8 10 9 7 5

POOH!
IS THAT YOU, BERTIE?

David Roberts

LITTLE TIGER PRESS
London

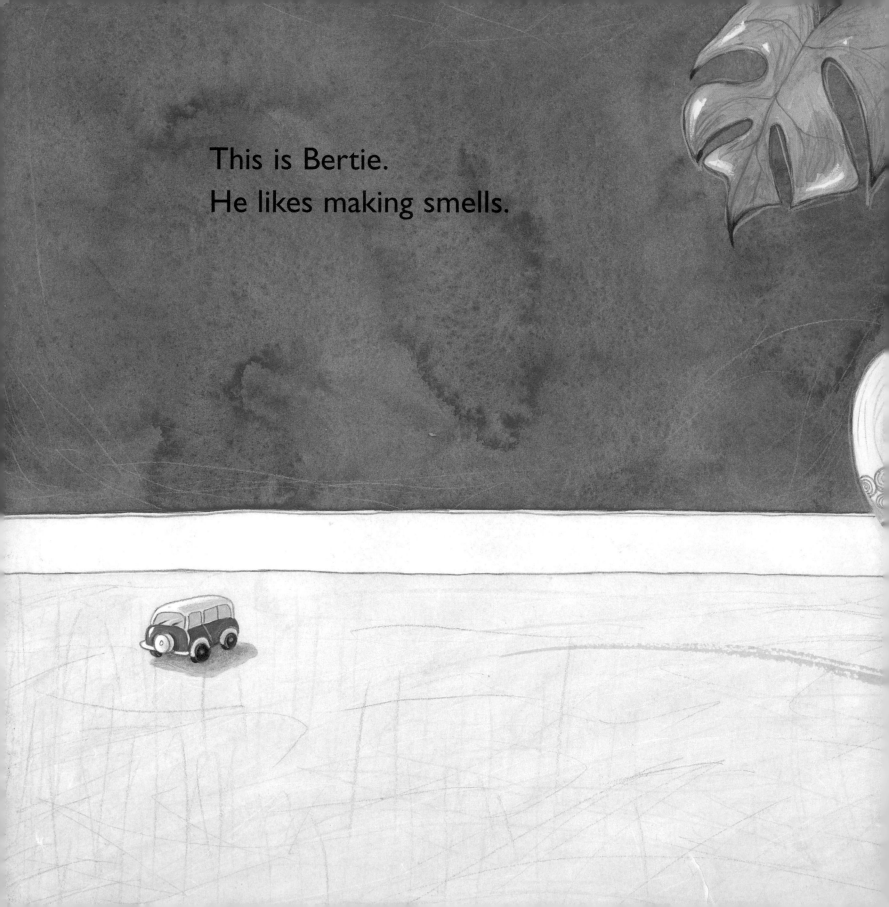

This is Bertie.
He likes making smells.

At the dentist Bertie let off a little poot.
It ponged.

"POOH!

IS THAT YOU, BERTIE?

That's not polite,"
sniffed Mum.

PARP

Bertie let off a big parp in the art gallery
and giggled. No one else did. It ponged.

"POOH!

IS THAT YOU, BERTIE?

I've never been so embarrassed,"
sniffed Dad.

At the café Bertie let off a smelly boff.
It ponged worse than a bad egg.

BOFF

"POOH!

IS THAT YOU, BERTIE?

It's not nice to break wind in the café,
not when people are eating,"
sniffed Gran.

Bertie let rip a tremendous trump in big sister Suzy's playhouse. It ponged. Suzy was livid.

"POOH!

IS THAT YOU, BERTIE?

You stink, smelly pants,"
sniffed Suzy.

It's not fair! thought Bertie.
I'm not the only one who stinks.

When Mum lets off a poot, she coughs
at the same time to cover it up.

When Dad lets off he's so sneaky...

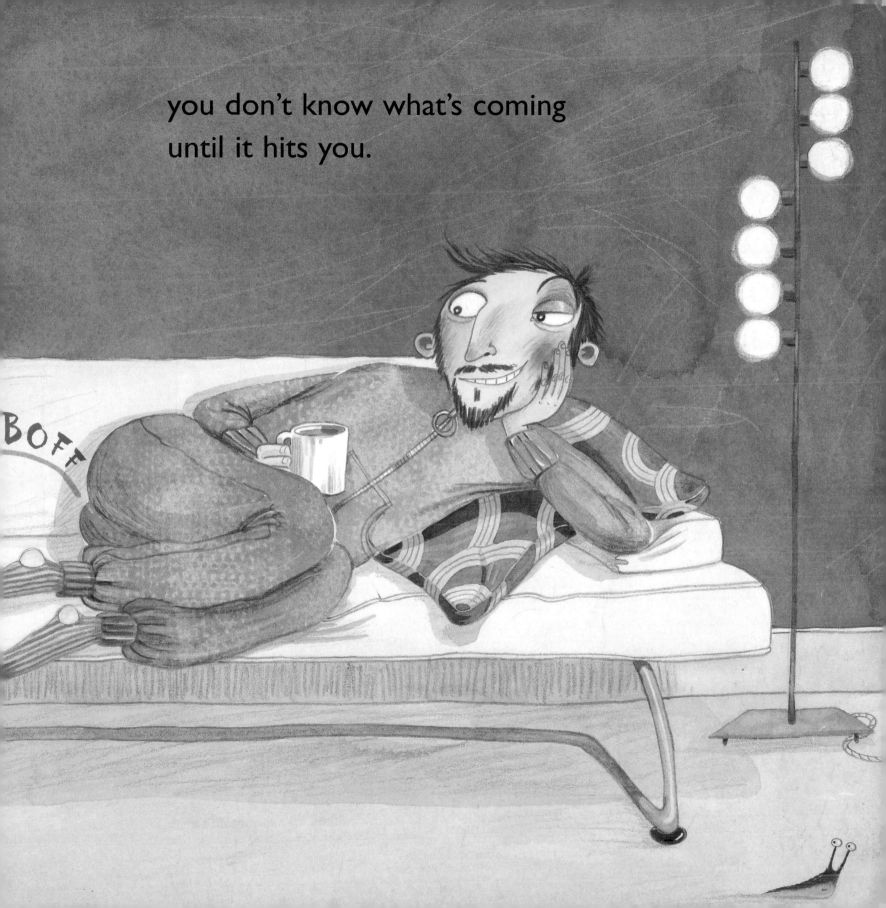

Gran's always letting rip.
She just blames the cat.

Suzy claims she never trumps.
But she sounds like a brass band
when she thinks no one's listening!

PRRRRP

FRRRP

PARP

And when the dog boffs,
he wafts it about!

POOOFF

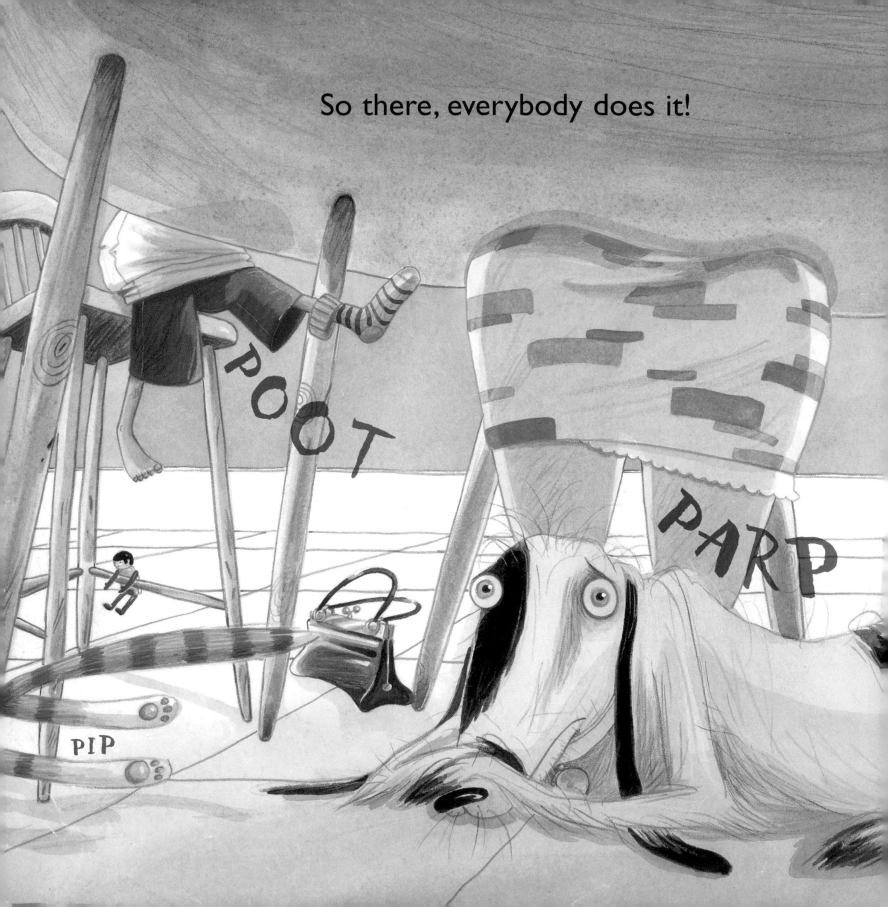

So there, everybody does it!

But *I* do it best . . .

Especially in the bath!

Stinking good books from Little Tiger Press!

For information regarding any of the above titles
or for our catalogue, please contact us:
Little Tiger Press, 1 The Coda Centre,
189 Munster Road, London SW6 6AW
Tel: 020 7385 6333 Fax: 020 7385 7333
Email: info@littletiger.co.uk
www.littletigerpress.com